SINDHU AND JEET'S DETECTIVE AGENCY

ACC. No: 07090660

SINDHU AND JEET'S DETECTIVE AGENCY

CHITRA SOUNDAR

ILLUSTRATED BY **AMBERIN HUQ**

BLOOMSBURY EDUCATION

LONDON OXFORD NEW YORK NEW DELHI SYDNEY

BLOOMSBURY EDUCATION
Bloomsbury Publishing Plc
50 Bedford Square, London, WC1B 3DP, UK
29 Earlsfort Terrace, Dublin 2, Ireland

BLOOMSBURY, BLOOMSBURY EDUCATION and the Diana logo are trademarks of
Bloomsbury Publishing Plc

First published in Great Britain in 2021 by Bloomsbury Publishing Plc

Text copyright © Chitra Soundar, 2021
Illustrations copyright © Amberin Huq, 2021

Chitra Soundar and Amberin Huq have asserted their rights under the Copyright, Designs
and Patents Act, 1988, to be identified as Author and Illustrator of this work

This is a work of fiction. Names and characters are the product of the author's
imagination and any resemblance to actual persons, living or dead, is entirely coincidental.

All rights reserved. No part of this publication may be reproduced or transmitted in any
form or by any means, electronic or mechanical, including photocopying, recording,
or any information storage or retrieval system, without prior permission in writing
from the publishers

A catalogue record for this book is available from the British Library

ISBN: PB: 978-1-4729-9331-1; ePDF: 978-1-4729-9333-5; ePub: 978-1-4729-9332-8

2 4 6 8 10 9 7 5 3 1

Cover and text design by Laura Neate

Printed and bound in the UK by CPI Group Ltd, CR0 4YY

MIX
Paper from
responsible sources
FSC® C020471

To find out more about our authors and books visit www.bloomsbury.com and sign up
for our newsletters

CONTENTS

ALL ABOARD

The dimly lit boarding gate at Chennai International Airport smelt of bleach. Sindhu flipped through the pages of her book – *The Handbook for Young Detectives* – and put it away.

She was going on a holiday to London with her parents, and most importantly her best friend Jeet, for a whole week. Yay! The trouble was that Jeet actually wanted to do sightseeing in London while Sindhu wanted to solve mysteries. They were, after all, Sindhu and Jeet's Detective Agency.

According to her book, detectives almost never went on holidays. Even if they did, they were pulled into solving mysteries. Also, detectives preferred flying business class where they had the space to discuss clues and interview suspects if they needed to do so. If only her parents could afford to fly them business class!

Mum and Dad were snoozing, catching up on sleep since they had had to leave for the airport at two in the morning. Jeet was playing with his new gadget – the latest model of pen-shaped spy-cam with *still, audio and video capabilities* (his words).

"Jeet!" Sindhu called, waving a folded sheet of paper. "Guess what this is?"

Jeet shrugged.

"The commendation letter from our headteacher Mrs Kandasamy for solving mysteries at the school."

"Why did you bring that?"

"Just in case we get to solve mysteries on the holiday!"

Jeet rolled his eyes. "No way," he insisted. "I'm going to be a tourist! Not a detective, for the next one week."

Let's see about that, thought Sindhu, carefully putting the letter in her jacket pocket and pulling out her OWL – Observation and Watch Log. The motto of every detective, according to *The Handbook for Young Detectives*, was Observe, Watch and Log.

"Say cheese!" shouted Jeet. "You're the 100th photo!"

Sindhu made a face at the camera and started logging her observations. Every entry had three sections.

#	who	where	what
1	a friend/detective turned photographer with a pen-camera	in the opposite seat	taking useless photos of the waiting area
2	a female cleaner wearing a sari, but with a blue uniform shirt over it	near the ladies' toilet	pushing a cleaning cart away from the toilet
3	a male cleaner dressed in the uniform blue shirt and in blue trousers	behind the female cleaner	sweeping the floor
4	airline staff — one with a long ponytail, the other with short hair	at the boarding counter	typing, laughing
5	everyone else	in uncomfortable bucket chairs	sleeping, dozing, snoozing, taking useless photos

"Sindhu!" called Jeet. "Please can you get your dad's phone?"

"Why?"

"This camera connects to a phone via a USB," explained Jeet. "So we can look at the pictures, sound recording or videos."

"Never wake a snoozing dad or a sleeping bear," said Sindhu, "if you want to live long enough to see London."

Jeet giggled as he turned away to take more pictures. Sindhu returned to her observation subjects. The cleaner man was gone. The cleaner woman was just pretending to wipe the door. She was looking in another direction completely.

Sindhu's detective instinct went on high alert. Something was not right. She needed to gather evidence. But if she asked Jeet to help, he would refuse. So, she needed a ruse.

"Jeet, how about a holiday project?"

"About what?"

"About professions around the world," said Sindhu. "Look! You can start with that cleaner."

"Genius!" said Jeet, turning on his camera to record the woman. "I'll record a video."

The PA system crackled. "We will begin boarding in the next ten minutes," the staff announced in three languages.

Passengers woke up from their slumber and started moving towards the boarding gate, blocking Jeet's view.

"I need to get closer," said Jeet as he walked ahead.

Sindhu followed him.

"The cleaner, she's gone," said Jeet.

"Wait!" said Sindhu. "What's that?"

"Some rag," said Jeet.

"Not any rag," said Sindhu. "It's her cleaning cloth."

"Oh no, careless cleaner," mocked Jeet. "I'll find another cleaner in London who isn't as careless. It's time to board. Come on!"

"Maybe she's just around the corner," said Sindhu, pulling Jeet with her.

"Sindhu!" called Mum. "Don't go far."

As they turned a corner, they bumped into the cleaning cart.

"That's strange!" said Sindhu.

"No, it's not," said Jeet. "Please don't imagine a mystery. She must be on her break or something."

*

The hall was busier. Sindhu and Jeet spotted a few cleaners dressed in blue shirts over saris. But none of them were the woman they had seen before.

"If she's on a break," said Sindhu, "she must be in the STAFF ONLY room."

"Doesn't matter," said Jeet. "I don't want to miss our holiday because we went looking for a cleaner on a toilet break."

But Sindhu had already opened the door and entered the cleaning closet marked STAFF ONLY.

It was lined with metal shelves filled with cleaning products, bins and rolls of bin liners. In one corner, a pantry was set up with a tray of empty glass tumblers, a kettle and some mugs for tea.

"You never listen!" hissed Jeet as he followed her inside. "Look! It's a cleaning closet. There's nothing else."

"Shh! Listen."

"What?"

"Can't you hear voices?"

They moved closer to the wall on the opposite side of the room. Garbled sounds came from the other side.

Jeet pulled Sindhu towards the door.

"Hang on!" whispered Sindhu. She tiptoed to the pantry and picked two glass tumblers. Jeet sighed and took one glass from her hand.

Sindhu placed the open side of her tumbler flat on the wall and pressed her right ear to its bottom. Jeet did the same. Then he had an idea. He held up his spy-cam near the tumbler too.

They could hear clearly what was being said on the other side. It was like magic! But really it was science – the resonance of the air waves through the glass.

"We need four bags – the easier to open the better, anything that will open with the universal luggage key."

"Boarding has started!" said a woman's voice. "We must hurry."

Whoever was on the other side was going to steal from passengers' luggage. Sindhu and Jeet's Detective Agency needed to stop them.

Then they heard a new voice, speaking in a hoarse whisper.

Sindhu leaned in closer, pushing

hard on the glass pressed against the wall.

CLICK!

Uh oh! She had pressed too hard. The wall wasn't a wall. It was a room divider. And now she was falling… down. Jeet tried to pull her back. But gravity was stronger than him. That was also not magic, just science.

Down she went. Sindhu braced for the fall. But she fell on something soft. Luggage.

THUMP! Jeet fell right next to her. Their glasses clattered to the floor.

"Hello there," a gruff man's voice called.

"Snooping, are we?" said the woman. The cleaner they had been searching for.

Sindhu and Jeet struggled to their feet, balancing on the wobbly bags. The woman got hold of Sindhu and the man grabbed Jeet.

"Lock them up until the job is done," the third man whispered. "Then make sure they get on that flight. Missing children will ruin all our plans to get rich."

"Yes boss!"

When the boss man turned and left, Sindhu saw her chance. "Now!" she hissed and kicked the woman's shins.

"Ow!" The woman let go of Sindhu.

The man tried to help the woman and loosened his hold on Jeet. Jeet broke free and they both ran through the door to find the boss man.

"Which way?" asked Jeet.

Sindhu looked to her left and right.

"That way is the runway, so he must have gone this side, maybe," said Sindhu. "Come on!"

They sprinted through the long corridor looking for an exit. Behind them, the fake cleaners were giving chase.

*

The corridor was so long, with a short roof like a tunnel. When they reached the other end, Sindhu and Jeet had to stop.

"We're trapped," said Jeet.

"Between a wall and two baggage burglars," said Sindhu.

The two cleaners slowed down to a stroll with evil grins on their faces.

"No bag or snooping children can escape from us," shouted the man.

The woman laughed.

"Maybe we can jump over the walls, over their heads and escape through the cleaning closet again," whispered Sindhu.

"Not unless we can magically turn into martial arts experts."

"We've got to do something," said Sindhu.

"We're not superheroes," said Jeet. "But we do play Kabadi."

Sindhu high-fived Jeet. That would work.

Both Sindhu and Jeet belonged to their school Kabadi team. Kabadi was a game of getting away. It was a bit like rugby but without the ball. You had to enter the opposing team's area, touch someone on their team and leave without being caught.

"We enter the domain of the cleaners," said Sindhu.

"And we leave without getting caught," said Jeet. "Just like a Kabadi match."

Sindhu nodded.

"1, 2, 3," Jeet counted.

Sindhu and Jeet ran headlong towards the cleaners, then quickly turned, ducked and rolled on the

ground, confusing the two cleaners.
An element of surprise was always
necessary for escape, their coach
always said. And it worked.

The woman tripped on her own
sari and fell. The man tried to stop her
from falling and tumbled on top of her.

Sindhu and Jeet ran through the corridor towards the cleaning closet. But it was blocked by the boss man.

"Over here!" called Jeet, running to the wall diagonally opposite. Jeet punched a square frame on the wall and it swung inwards. It was a hatch.

"Good observation!" shouted Sindhu as Jeet pulled himself into the hatch. She quickly followed.

Aaagh! They were sliding down on something rubbery.

"Why do they have slides inside an airport?" asked Jeet.

"And why didn't they tell the kids?" asked Sindhu.

BRRDDRRR!

What was that?

Their rubber slide juddered and shook. Suddenly they started to move faster. Their legs pushed through flaps of rubber.

Aaaaaaghh!

Tumbling on top of suitcases and bags on the baggage carousel, they arrived into the arrivals hall.

"We're a week early," quipped Jeet.

"Jump!" shouted Sindhu.

"Move the trolleys," Jeet shouted to the passengers waiting for their luggage. But the momentum of the carousel made it impossible to land gracefully on their feet.

"Ugh! Phenol," said Jeet as they hit the floor.

"And bleach with a lemon fragrance," said Sindhu.

They were pulled up by a very stern security guard. "What in the name of the god of travel are you doing on the carousel?" he shouted. "Where did you arrive from?"

"We're not arriving," shouted Sindhu. "We're leaving. Our flight is boarding right now."

"That's unfortunate," said the guard. "Once you're in the arrivals hall, you need a new ticket to go back to departures."

"But we were trying to stop a robbery!" said Jeet.

The guard hustled them into a dingy office and pointed at two chairs without a smile. Then he rapidly spoke into a walkie-talkie.

"Playing detectives?" he asked.

Sindhu showed him her OWL. "Look!"

"Good handwriting," the guard said.

"Here!" said Sindhu, pulling out the commendation letter she had brought with her. "We really are detectives."

"I'm not buying any of this. The truth please! Otherwise, we're cancelling your holiday and calling the police."

"We have real proof," said Jeet.

Before the guard could answer, Sindhu's parents came running into the room.

"Are you OK?" shouted Mum.

"What have you done now?" asked Dad.

"Can I borrow your phone, Mani Uncle?" asked Jeet.

Sindhu's dad handed the phone to Jeet and Jeet plugged his spy-cam into it.

The first hundred photos were photos of the airport.

"I'm still not seeing any real proof as you promised," said the guard.

"Look!" screamed Sindhu as the

cleaner's face came into focus. "She's one of them."

"She's just a cleaner," said the guard.

"Wait until you hear this," said Jeet, turning up the volume on the phone.

He replayed the conversation he had recorded using the glass tumbler, before Sindhu had fallen through the wall.

But it was just garble.

"Really?" said the guard. "This is your proof?"

"Wait!" said Jeet. "I left the recording running, so you'll hear everything they said to us."

As promised a video played, showing the three thieves threatening them and mentioning getting rich, the sound crisp and clear.

"Hmm," said the guard. "OK... That's interesting."

"See, real proof," said Sindhu. "We're real detectives."

The guard rushed out, talking into a walkie-talkie.

Mum and Dad checked their watches a million times. Sindhu tried not to look them in the eyes. They were going to miss the holiday because of her.

At last, the guard returned to the office. "We've got them," he said, "when they were trying to open some suitcases for another flight. Thank you for being alert!"

Sindhu smiled. *Our holiday has been sacrificed for a good cause,* she thought.

The PA system crackled. "Last call for Flight A73 to London."

"Oh no!" said Mum. "We're going to miss our flight."

"Our tickets are non-refundable," said Dad.

"Sorry!" said Sindhu. "It's all my fault."

"We stopped a burglary though," said Jeet.

"We're just happy you're safe," said Mum.

"Don't worry," said the guard. "We're holding the flight for you."

He led them back to the boarding gate.

The airline staff welcomed them with big smiles.

"Jeet and I are in 27 E and F," said Sindhu, as they entered the plane.

"No, you're not," said the flight attendant. "We've upgraded you to business class, as a small thank you for catching the burglars."

Mum smiled at Sindhu and Jeet. "Thanks to Sindhu and Jeet's Detective Agency!"

"Hear, hear!" said Dad.

"Let's hope the rest of the holiday is quiet," said Jeet.

"Maybe!" said Sindhu, crossing her fingers behind her back. Quiet holidays were boring.

BUILDING BRIDGES

It was the first day of their London holiday.

"After breakfast, let's go for a walk along the riverside, I'm told it's historic," said Mum.

"Only until Dad gets tickets for the Tower of London," said Sindhu.

Dad pulled out his phone and checked. "Those tickets are way too expensive."

"Dad!" cried Sindhu. "We HAVE to see the Crown Jewels. I want to see the ravens too."

"There are crows in India!" said Dad.

"Actually, the crows in Chennai are jackdaws," said Jeet.

"Come on, Dad," said Sindhu. "We have to go to the Tower of London."

"Fine! Go on your walk and I'll get the tickets," said Dad. "Meet you by that tunnel?"

"Just get them online," said Mum.

"I want to show them all the free coupons and find the best price for the tickets."

Right outside the hotel, there were display boards explaining the history of Tower Bridge, the river and how it brought ships from India, China and many other countries.

"Do you think we can go on top of Tower Bridge?" Jeet asked. "I bet the river looks pretty from up there."

"Don't know," said Sindhu.

Before they could venture east, Dad returned with the tickets. "There was a long line," he said, "and this woman almost tried to cut me off. But I held my ground."

"Did you get the tickets, Dad?" asked Sindhu.

"Yes, and they were almost a third cheaper."

"Oh good!" said Mum. "Now everyone's happy. Let's go."

But as they walked through the tunnel, Dad started climbing the steps to the bridge. Uh oh! Sindhu knew something was wrong. The Tower of London was to their right.

"Come on!" said Dad. "It's up there."

"Mani!" Mum said. "I think you've got the wrong tickets."

Even though Dad had got it wrong, he insisted they use the tickets.

"But Dad," Sindhu moaned.

"It was meant to be," said Mum. "We can see the river from up there, just like Jeet wanted."

"I wanted to see the Tower too," said Jeet.

Sindhu refused to talk to her dad as they got into the lift.

"Hey!" Dad whispered. "That's the woman who was trying to cut the queue."

Even though she didn't want to, Sindhu instinctively looked. That's what detectives did. She pulled out her OWL and logged it in.

#	who	where	what
1	a tall woman with wide shoulders, her hair in a ponytail	in the lift	she cut the queue in front of Dad

The lift stopped on the exhibition floor.

"We're standing 44 metres above the river," said Jeet.

"Look!" said Dad, pointing at a sign. "That's 206 steps to the ground level."

"Heroes of the Bridge!" Mum read aloud from the posters. "This is all about the people who worked on the bridge. Mani, look! There was an Indian engineer working here too."

Dad put on his glasses and peered at the poster. "Keshavji Shamji Budhbhatti."

"I'm bored already," said Sindhu.

"Don't be like that," said Mum.

"We're in London for a week. We can go to the Tower some other time. Just enjoy this now."

Jeet was definitely enjoying it. He took out his spy-cam and held it to the windows and took photos of the river, the river birds and the police boats.

"Jeet!" called Sindhu. "Do you want to play Count the Objects?" she asked.

"No thanks!" said Jeet. "Detective Jeet is on holiday."

"Fine!" said Sindhu. She'd do it on her own.

Count the Objects was simple – observe, count and log.

1 – bin on each side at each end

2 – people with coloured hair – 1 purple, 1 orange

3 – staff members

4 – people with big coats

5 – people wearing hats

6 – radiators – 3 on each side

7 – little kids running around shouting

8 – people with cameras with zoom lens

9 – photos on each side of the walkway in the exhibition

"Sindhu," called Mum. "Look! We can see the bridge through the glass floor."

Jeet came over. "Can we take a Sindhu and Jeet's Detective Agency selfie please?"

"Sure!" said Sindhu. "As long as the caption reads *Famous Detectives in*

London when you put it up on your blog."

They stood against the backdrop of the river as Jeet held up his pen horizontally.

"Say cheese!" said Jeet.

That's when Sindhu noticed. Eight!

"Only eight," she said.

Jeet clicked the picture. "I've never heard anyone say 'Only Eight' instead of 'Cheese'."

"No, look, there are only eight photos on both sides," said Sindhu, opening her OWL. "There were nine before. I wrote it down."

"If I borrow your dad's phone," said Jeet, "I can confirm whether it was eight or nine."

Jeet plugged his pen into the phone and they flipped through the photos. There were a thousand photos of the river. But just a few of the walkway.

"Check that one," said Sindhu.

Jeet counted the framed photos captured in the panorama shot.

Nine!

"Hmm, maybe the staff removed them?" suggested Jeet.

"I don't think they'd remove them in the middle of an exhibition," said Sindhu. "These are photos of people from the past. Why would anyone steal these?"

"Maybe the frames were more valuable," said Jeet.

Sindhu nodded. That could be it. But how would the thief carry the two frames out?

"Show me your Count the Objects list," said Jeet, pulling the OWL from her hand. "Here! You counted four people wearing big coats. It's summer. Why would anyone wear a long coat?"

"Unless they wanted to smuggle out frames," said Sindhu.

Three out of the four people wearing long coats were in a group. "You watch them," said Jeet. "I'll watch that other guy."

The group of long-coat people moved slowly, reading every poster. They seemed genuinely interested in the exhibition. Sindhu observed their coat pockets. None of them sagged, weighed down by frames.

"I don't think it's them," said Sindhu said. "What about your guy?"

"He does behave suspiciously, holding his coat tight all the time," said Jeet.

Sindhu and Jeet stood behind him, pretending to look at the portraits he was looking at.

The man suddenly turned to Sindhu with a big smile.

"It's so cold, isn't it?" he said. "I'm used to 35 degrees heat."

Sindhu and Jeet nodded and smiled a little.

"Red herring," said Sindhu, walking backwards from the man.

"Watch out," said Jeet, a little too late, as she bumped into a woman taking a selfie.

"Did you know over 250 people die every year taking a selfie?" asked Jeet.

Sindhu scowled. "It's that woman who tried to cut Dad off in the line."

The woman put her selfie-stick away and walked towards the exit. She then crouched on the ground as if to tie her shoelaces and dropped something into the bin.

"Did you see that?" asked Sindhu.

"Let's check the bin," said Jeet, moving quickly through the crowd towards the bin. Sindhu caught up with him.

A photo frame sat in the bin with a photo in it. Sindhu tried to reach for it.

"Don't," said Jeet. "It'll have her fingerprints on it."

"There's only one frame," said Sindhu. "Where's the other one?"

"That's the one she stole," said Jeet.

"But if the frames are expensive, why would she leave this behind?" asked Sindhu.

Jeet nodded. "Yes, all the frames in the exhibition are identical. Including the one in the bin."

CRACKLE! The PA system announced that the lift was ready to go down. The woman quickly moved towards the lift.

"We must follow her," shouted Sindhu. Too many people pushed past them into the lift and they couldn't get in.

"Let's take the stairs," said Sindhu to Jeet. "Meet you downstairs, Mum."

Mum quickly gave her backpack to Dad. "I'm going with Sindhu," she said. "Need to get more steps in today anyway."

Sindhu scampered down the steps, followed by Jeet and Mum.

Just as they reached the ground floor, the woman darted across the road, avoiding a cyclist.

"Quick, let's take the tunnel to cross the road," said Jeet. "It's faster."

"Wait!" cried Mum. "What's going on?"

"Run with us," shouted Sindhu. "I'll explain."

As Jeet ran ahead down the steps to the bottom of the bridge, Sindhu explained to Mum between breathing and running. "That woman – stole photo from exhibition – we saw – we want to catch…"

"OK!" said Mum. "Let's get her."

Sindhu laughed aloud. "You're the best mum ever," she said.

They were on street level to the south of the river. Which way had that woman gone?

"There!" shouted Jeet and dashed ahead.

"STOP!" shouted Sindhu.

The woman ran down the street filled with tourists and shops on either side. The pavement was too crowded and the street was cobbled, so Sindhu, Jeet and Mum soon caught up.

Just as Sindhu was at arm's length, the woman turned right into a street that had more buildings named after spices than Sindhu's grandmother's spice cupboard. Sindhu, Jeet and Mum dashed after her.

The woman dashed left and right as if she knew the streets really well. Then she slowed down and stopped near a full-size horse sculpture in the middle of the road.

Just as Sindhu had almost caught up with her, the woman shot out from behind the statue like an arrow from a bow. But this time, Sindhu was losing ground.

"Come on," said Jeet. "We don't want her to escape."

Sindhu followed Jeet as Mum kept pace with her.

The street led them back to the river.

"We're going in circles," cried Sindhu.

"Look," cried Jeet. "We're in Jacob's Island. Look at the blue plaque."

Just for a second, Sindhu turned to see the big blue plaque. When they turned back to the street, the woman was gone.

"There!" shouted Mum, spotting the woman running through a narrow alley to cross over a private bridge. But unfortunately, the bridge was busy and she couldn't get on it.

Mum's phone rang. Mum explained the situation to Dad as fast and as coherently as she could, which went something like – "Woman steal photo, call police, by the river, Jacob's Island."

The bridge was now clear. The woman hurried over it.

"Now!" cried Jeet.

"Go! Go!" shouted Sindhu.

Sindhu and Jeet dashed across. Mum followed. Fortunately for them and unfortunately for the woman, a family of six with two twin pushchairs was coming from the other side.

The photo thief was trapped between three tourists who were chasing her and the two pushchairs.

"It'll be funny if we catch her and she doesn't have the photo," said Jeet.

"What?" cried Mum. "I thought you were chasing a criminal, so I asked Dad to call the police…"

THUMP!

"Oh dear!" said Mum.

The woman had jumped from the bridge onto the riverbed.

"The tide's out," said Jeet. "Maybe…"

"No, don't you dare!" said Mum, reading their minds. "The hotel laundry will charge me an entire month's salary."

Fortunately for them and unfortunately for the woman, the police boats arrived right on time with Dad.

"Well done, Dad," shouted Sindhu.

Two police officers jumped over on to the riverbed and caught the woman.

One officer dug into the woman's bag and pulled out a photo in its frame.

Sindhu and Jeet inched forward. "Excuse me," said Sindhu. "Why did you steal that photo?"

The woman glared at them.

"We know you didn't take it for the frame," said Jeet.

The woman smiled sadly.

"Was it the photo of someone you love?" asked Mum.

The woman shook her head. "No! I don't know who is in the photo."

The police officer frowned. "So why did you steal it?" she asked.

The woman broke down in tears. "That was the last photo my great-grandad ever took and developed with his own hands. I asked the exhibition curators to give me the original. But they wouldn't."

"Oh no!" said Sindhu. "Sorry we scuppered your plan."

"I'm sorry too," said Jeet.

"But the end doesn't justify the means," said the police officer as she led the woman into the first boat. "You're under arrest."

"There's value in old photos," said Dad. "With this digital stuff, you guys take random stuff with no forethought."

Jeet laughed. "Isn't that great?"

"Let's go back to the hotel and rest up," said Dad. "Too much excitement for one morning."

"We can give you a lift across the river, if you want," said the officer.

"Yay! We'll get to ride in a police boat," said Sindhu. "Like real detectives."

"We are real detectives," said Jeet.

"But I really want to go to the Tower though," said Sindhu.

"Of course!" said Dad. "I'll get the tickets online this time, so I don't get it wrong again."

"Hang on!" said the officer. "We can drop you off at the Tower and then how about we call in for some complimentary tickets, if you'd like. As a thank you for helping to fight crime."

"Oh wow!" said Sindhu. "Yes please."

"Thank you," said Jeet.

"That's amazing!" said Dad. "This visit to the Tower is sponsored by the London Police."

"Actually, it's sponsored by Sindhu and Jeet's Detective Agency," said Mum.

Everyone laughed.

A HARD SHELL TO CRACK

After their trip to the Tower of London and then a day of rest, it was time to visit the Natural History Museum. Everyone had a list of things they wanted to see. Especially Mum, who was super keen to see the museum's conch collection.

"So, your mum is a conch expert?" asked Jeet.

"She is a collector and an expert," said Sindhu. "Did you know this special type of conch she collects is only found in the Indian Ocean? Most temples in India have one and some of the big ones are worth millions."

"Millions for a conch!" Jeet exclaimed.

Inside the museum they decided to split up.

The kids are with me," said Dad. "And Mum is…"

"…going to see the conch section," finished Sindhu.

"I'm so excited to see their rare Valampuri Sangu from the Indian Ocean."

"How do you identify it?" asked Jeet.

"Oh dear!" said Dad with a chuckle. "Stand by for a lecture now!"

"There are three distinct markers," said Mum in her documentary voice. "Firstly, it belongs to the family of Turbinella pyrum [as if they were all supposed to know what that was]. Secondly, the spiral of the conch must twist right-side. Thirdly, some of them will have the twist right-side and downwards."

"Go on then," said Dad. "Go to your shell section."

"The marine invertebrate section," said Mum. "Meet you back at the café for lunch?"

"Can I come with you?" asked Sindhu, "to see the conch?"

"Of course," said Mum.

"The boys will head to the bones then," said Dad.

Mum and Sindhu linked their arms together and Mum continued where she had left off on the lecture.

"Our ancient epics talk about these in detail," said Mum. "The one your dad uses for his morning prayers has been handed down for generations. It was found in Kanya Kumari, the southernmost tip of our country."

When they reached the Marine Invertebrates hall, Mum checked the chart on the wall and headed straight to the display cabinet marked I0-A1. But the cabinet was empty. A sign said

> **THIS ARTEFACT HAS BEEN REMOVED TEMPORARILY.**

"This room is cold," said Sindhu. "Let's go out and see something else."

"Here, take my jacket," her mum replied, not moving from the display case. "Don't leave the pockets open. My phone is in there."

"OK," said Sindhu. "But are we staying here long if the conch isn't on display?"

"Yeah, I'm going to wander a bit and see the other displays. Don't leave the room, darling."

"OK!" said Sindhu, looking at the displays in the Crustacean and Mollusca collections.

Suddenly a shrill voice broke the whispered chatter in the room. Her mum's shrill voice. Mum was arguing with a woman with a museum badge. Uh oh!

Sindhu hurried over.

"Miss Finch, you don't understand," said Mum. "This is not a Valampuri Sangu." Mum was pointing at the glass case, where a conch had been put back instead of the REMOVED sign.

People hovered to watch the tourist shout at a member of the museum staff. Mum took out her magnifying glass and peered at the displayed conch.

"See, this spiral here," said Mum.

Miss Finch came closer. "You must be mistaken," she said.

Sindhu went to Mum's other side. The spiral on the shell was shaped upwards to the left.

"This is not a Valampuri Sangu," insisted Mum.

"I'll look into this right away," said Miss Finch, half-smiling and moving away to the door.

"I need to find someone to complain to," said Mum.

"Can you do that after lunch?" asked Sindhu. "I'm starving."

*

When Sindhu and Mum arrived at the café, Dad and Jeet were already seated. Jeet was playing with his pen-camera.

"The food's so expensive here," said Dad, reading the menu.

But Sindhu and Jeet were too hungry to worry about prices. They went to the counter to gawk at the cakes.

"Did something happen?" asked Jeet. "Your mum looks upset."

Sindhu explained the conch story to him.

"But why would they mislabel it?" asked Jeet.

Sindhu shrugged.

Just as they turned back to the table, Miss Finch came into the café.

"Look!" whispered Sindhu. "That's her."

Miss Finch picked up a tray and pulled out the chair just behind Mum.

"Uh oh!" said Sindhu.

"Let's go and change table before your mum makes a big scene," said Jeet.

"If there's a fight, my mum will definitely win," said Sindhu. "Especially about…"

Sindhu spotted something and pulled Jeet back.

"…conches?" asked Jeet.

Sindhu pointed at Miss Finch. The woman had turned around and was digging into Mum's bag, which was hanging behind her chair. Mum hadn't noticed.

"Mum!" shouted Sindhu.

Jeet darted ahead with his camera recording.

Miss Finch looked up. She lifted her empty tray and threw it at Jeet, who ducked so the tray came flying at Sindhu, who also ducked. The tray sailed and crashed into an arrangement of brownies behind them at the dessert counter. Someone screamed.

Miss Finch fled from the café, clattering plates and pushing chairs on her way out.

"Go go go!" shouted Sindhu.

They chased Miss Finch, swerving around pushchairs, little children and people with maps.

"Watch it!" shouted Jeet, as Sindhu almost ran into a donation box near the entrance.

Miss Finch was nearing the exit. Sindhu shouted to the guards. "Catch her! Miss Finch! Stop!"

Miss Finch slowed down as the guards stopped her and pointed at Sindhu.

"What did you take from my mum's bag?" demanded Sindhu.

"Daphne, any problems?" asked the guard.

"No, nothing, Jimmy," replied Miss Daphne Finch. "I'll take care of it."

Miss Finch pulled Sindhu to a quiet corner.

"Hey! Leave her be," shouted Jeet.

"Shut up!" hissed Miss Finch. "I didn't take anything from your mother. Look!" She opened her bag and tipped it out.

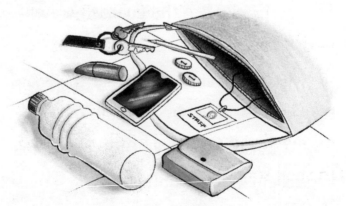

She was telling the truth. None of that was Mum's stuff.

As Sindhu and Jeet watched silently, Miss Finch gathered her things and stomped out of the building, her heels click-clacking on the marble floor.

"What just happened?" asked Jeet. "Maybe we interrupted her before she could take anything."

"Why would one of the museum staff steal from a tourist?" asked Sindhu.

As they walked back, Sindhu said, "This is what we know about her. Firstly, she works in the marine invertebrate section. Secondly, she mislabelled a conch. Thirdly, she tried to steal something."

"Hang on," said Jeet. "What if she wasn't stealing, what if she was putting something in?"

"We must check Mum's bag," said Sindhu. "Hurry!"

But Sindhu's parents weren't in the café.

TRRRRING!

"You're ringing," said Jeet, pointing at her jacket.

"Oh! Mum's phone," said Sindhu.

It was Dad calling. "Come to the marine invertebrates hall," said Dad. "There's an office next to the entrance. I'm standing there."

"Oh dear! Has Mum filed a complaint?"

"No, the other way round," said Dad. "Come quickly."

*

Dad stood outside the office looking super worried.

"What happened?" asked Sindhu. "Where's Mum?"

"We were eating lunch in the café when suddenly the security guards pounced on Mum and dragged her here."

"But why?"

"Apparently she stole the Valampuri Sangu," said Dad.

"That's not possible," said Sindhu.

"Did Mum touch the display when she was in the hall?"

"No!" said Sindhu. "The display case was empty at first. Then Miss Finch, that woman we were chasing, placed a conch inside the case. Mum said it wasn't the Valampuri Sangu and she got quite upset with Miss Finch."

"Oh no!" said Jeet. "I think… Do you know what I mean?"

Sindhu's eyes widened. "What if Miss Finch put the fake one on display and then put the real one in

Mum's bag? That's what she was doing in the café!"

"What are you talking about?"

"Aunty is being framed," said Jeet.

Dad scratched his head and took a deep breath. "OK, OK! We're tourists here. I'm going to call my lawyer friend first. You both sit here! Don't move."

As soon as Dad turned around, Sindhu whispered, "I've got to see Mum."

"How?" asked Jeet.

Sindhu took off Mum's jacket and walked up to the security guard. "I want to see my mum," she said.

"Sorry! You've to wait until Miss Finch gets here."

"But I have my mum's jacket," said Sindhu. "She'll be cold inside."

"Sorry!"

"It's a violation of her human rights," shouted Sindhu.

"Please keep your voice down," she said calmly, standing between Sindhu and the door.

Some visitors stopped to look. One man seemed keen to intervene.

"Fine!" said the guard. "You can go in with the jacket. Empty the pockets please."

Sindhu rolled her eyes as she handed Mum's phone to Jeet and pushed down the door handle.

"Sindhu," called Jeet.

"Your mum might need a pen," said Jeet, handing over his spy-cam. "In case she wants to sign a confession?"

The guard nodded and let Sindhu in.

The office was brightly lit. On the shelves were certificates claiming Miss Finch was a marine biologist. On the other end of the room was a tall mahogany cupboard.

Mum was seated on a wooden chair with her head on the table.

"Mum!" said Sindhu. "Are you OK? Don't be upset."

Mum looked up. "I'm not upset," she said. "I'm livid. First, she mislabels the conch and then she claims I've stolen it," hissed Mum. "How dare she!"

"She planted it in your bag, Mum," said Sindhu, "in the café. We thought she was stealing at first. But now…"

There was a sudden noise outside.

"Go and wait outside," said Mum. "I think she's here."

"I have a plan," said Sindhu. "Ask her why she did it, OK?"

Sindhu scrambled into the mahogany cupboard and shut the door behind her. She turned on the spy-cam and stuck it in front of the keyhole in the cupboard. She really hoped her plan was going to work.

Miss Finch entered with the security guard.

"Did you search her bags?" she asked.

"No, Miss Finch," said the guard. "We were told to wait for you and her lawyer to arrive."

"Only guilty people need lawyers," said Miss Finch, shutting the door behind her and sitting in front of Mum.

"So, you need one, right?" said Mum.

Sindhu almost chuckled. Her dad had always said Mum was the bravest person he had ever met and Sindhu understood why.

"Admit to the theft and hand over the conch!" shouted Miss Finch.

"I didn't steal anything!" said Mum. "You mislabelled the conch in the display. Did you buy that degree in a fake school?"

"Hey!" said Miss Finch. "I'm a real marine biologist. But I'm OK writing a wrong label here and there. Especially for a million pounds."

Miss Finch chuckled as if she was so proud of herself.

"Shame on you," said Mum in her

mum voice.

Miss Finch didn't reply. She took out a file and started writing.

"You mislabelled the fake and stole the real one to sell," said Mum. "But why did you put it in my bag? Why not just take it home yourself?"

"They always check staff bags," said Miss Finch, looking up. "So, I always pick a clueless tourist to carry something out for me. And then when you're taking some silly selfie outside, a little bird can fly away with your bag."

Sindhu inhaled sharply. How many times had Miss Finch stolen stuff from the museum? She had to be stopped.

Mum grunted. "Fine!" she said. "Good plan. Why didn't you wait for me to come out of the museum and steal it from me? Why did you report me? Did you get scared?"

Miss Finch laughed. "I don't get scared," she shouted. "I had to adapt because your silly daughter chased me around the museum. Things like that stick in guards' minds. So I decided to frame you, so no one will suspect me later."

"Oh wow!" said Mum. Sindhu was sure it was a sarcastic 'wow'. "Now what?"

"Why would I tell you?" said Miss Finch.

"So, you have no clue what to do now, right?" said Mum.

"Of course I know what to do," said Miss Finch with indignation. "I will confiscate the original from you now, swap it with a fake and sell the original."

"Oh wow!" said Mum.

This time it wasn't sarcastic. Because that was a good plan, Sindhu realised.

Even if years later someone found the fake, they'd come looking for Mum because she was the thief on record. She had to stop Miss Finch from stealing and framing her mum.

She jumped out of the cupboard shouting, "Gotcha!"

"What are YOU doing here?" shouted Miss Finch. "Security!" she called.

The door opened and Jeet burst in followed by the guard. Dad came in after them.

"Call Miss Finch's boss," said Sindhu. "Please!"

"Is everything OK in here, Miss Finch?" asked the security guard.

Miss Finch didn't stop to explain. She tried to make a break for it.

"Not so fast," said Jeet, casually extending his leg out to trip her and break her run.

Miss Finch fell face down on the carpeted floor with a thud.

When Mr Stanley Soda, Miss
Finch's boss, arrived, Mum explained
the million-pound plan to steal and sell
the conch.

"I don't believe it," he said. "Miss
Finch wouldn't do such a thing."

"But we can prove Miss Finch did
it," said Sindhu.

Jeet plugged the spy-cam into Dad's
phone and pressed Play.

The confession had been recorded fully and the replay audio and keyhole video were crisp and clear.

Mr Soda sighed loudly.

"I think Mr Soda has fizzled out," whispered Jeet.

Miss Finch was taken away and the rest, as they say, is Natural History.

Mum later got a private tour of the conch collections. The Museum gave them each a lifetime pass to everything, including the special exhibitions.

When they sat down for some tea and cake, Dad said, "I wish WE had sold the conch for a million pounds. It would have come in handy to pay for these cakes."

"After this, let's head to the special exhibitions," said Jeet. "We've more than an hour left before they close."

"Oh no! How much is that going to cost?" wailed Dad.

"It's free, Mani," said Mum, fanning herself with her lifetime pass.

"Courtesy of Sindhu and Jeet's Detective Agency!"

Sindhu laughed. Her holiday was going exactly as she had hoped. Not at all boring!

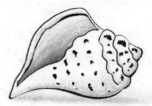